D0544985

For the children of Montserrat

First published 2005 by Walker Books Ltd
87 Vauxhall Walk, London SE11 5HJ

2 4 6 8 10 9 7 5 3 1

© 2005 Frané Lessac

The right of Frané Lessac to be identified as author/illustrator of this work has been
asserted by her in accordance with the Copyright, Designs and Patents Act 1988

This book has been typeset in Johann Bold

Printed in China

British Library Cataloguing in Publication Data:
a catalogue record for this book is available from the British Library

ISBN 1-84428-246-5

www.walkerbooks.co.uk

Island Counting
1 2 3

Frané Lessac

WALKER BOOKS
AND SUBSIDIARIES
LONDON · BOSTON · SYDNEY · AUCKLAND

One *little* island in

the Caribbean Sea.

1

Two parrots squawking

in a coconut tree.

Three painted houses

sitting high on a hill.

Four donkeys running

round the old sugar mill. **4**

Five market ladies

wearing shady hats.

Six cricket players

waiting with their bats.

Seven beach umbrellas

soaking up the sun.

7

Eight drummers drumming

– ping pa ping pom.

Nine limbo dancers

swaying in a line.

9

Ten children jump up and shout,

"Hooray, it's carnival time!" **10**

All on one little island

in the Caribbean Sea.

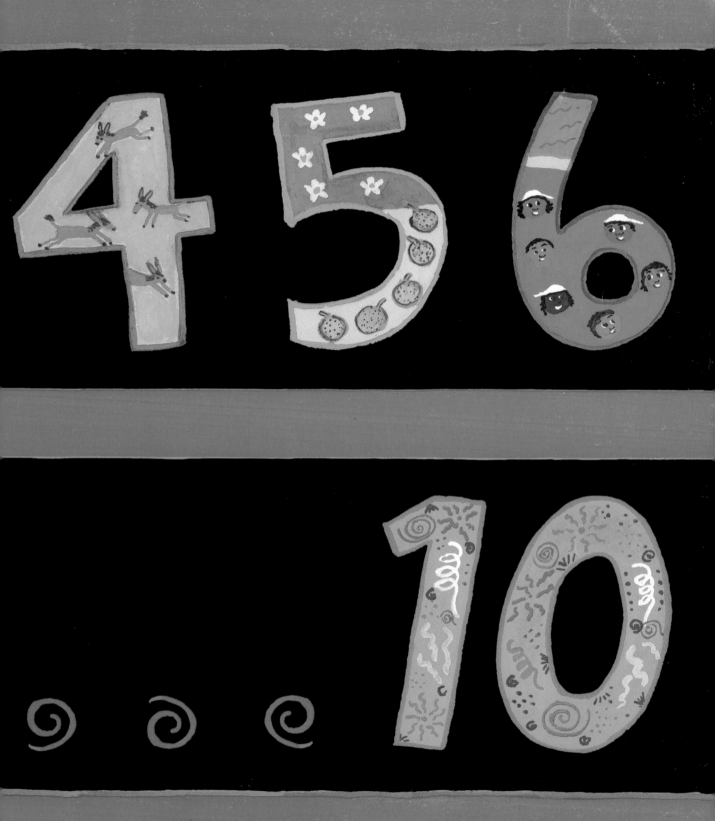

WALKER BOOKS is the world's leading
independent publisher of children's books.
Working with the best authors and illustrators
we create books for all ages, from babies
to teenagers – books your child will
grow up with and always remember. So…

FOR THE BEST CHILDREN'S BOOKS,
LOOK FOR THE BEAR